DISNEY'S

Snow White
and the Seven Dwarfs

FLEETWAY BOOKS

Once upon a time a beautiful young Princess lived with her father and mother, the King and Queen, in a faraway land. Her name was Snow White.

Alas! The Queen died and the King married again. The new Queen was beautiful, too, and she was also very jealous! She hated Snow White.

'You will now be my servant!' she cried.

Snow White had to obey her step-mother, the Queen, but she remained sweet, gentle and kind. All the birds of the air and the animals of the forest were her friends. The birds flew down to cheer her up as she washed and swept and scrubbed.

'One day Prince Charming will come to take you in his arms,' they said.

3

Each day the proud Queen spoke to the magic mirror in the palace:
'Mirror, mirror, on the wall,
'Who is the fairest of us all?'
she asked.
And the mirror replied:
'You are the fairest of all, O Queen,
The fairest our eyes have ever seen.'
But every day Snow White was growing more and more beautiful. And her step-mother the Queen grew more and more jealous of her.

One day, a handsome Prince came riding by the palace on a magnificent horse, just as the birds had said would happen. At sight of Snow White he fell on his knees and cried: 'Beautiful Princess, I love you! Tomorrow I will ask your father the King's permission to marry you!'

'But the Queen would never allow it, fair Prince!' sighed Snow White.

'Then I will carry you off!'

Snow White's heart leapt.

'Until tomorrow, Princess Snow White!' cried the Prince.

The Queen, who had seen and heard the Prince talking to Snow White, spoke to the mirror.
The mirror replied:
'Fair is thy beauty, Majesty,
But hold – a lovely maid I see,
One who is more fair than thee.
Lips red as rose, hair black as ebony,
Skin white as snow . . ."
'Snow White!' shrieked the angry Queen.
She sent for her huntsman.

The Queen ordered the huntsman to
take Snow White into the forest.
Snow White was sure her step-
mother really loved her – or else why
was she allowing her to take such a
lovely walk?
So she laughed and played happily
with her friends the birds.
She didn't know that the Queen had
told the huntsman that as soon as
they were deep in the forest he was to
kill Snow White!

The huntsman took out his knife and raised it, ready to strike down the Princess.

Snow White cried out for mercy and the huntsman, who was really a kind man, fell on his knees in dismay.

'Oh, Princess!' he cried. 'A thousand pardons! The Queen commanded me to kill you and to put your heart in this box. But I cannot do it.'

'She will kill you if you disobey her!' cried Snow White.

'Don't worry about me, Princess,' replied the huntsman. 'You must get away from the jealous Queen. You must flee into the forest, where your friends the birds and the animals will take care of you. Now go! Run! Save yourself!'

With her heart pounding, Snow White ran and ran, and she
didn't stop until night fell on the forest.
From the dark shadows strange eyes stared out at her.
Tangled branches tore at her clothes. Sharp twigs scratched
her arms and legs. Everywhere danger lurked.
Snow White fell wearily on the ground. 'My Prince will never
find me now!' she sobbed. And she cried herself to sleep.

When she woke up all the animals of the forest were gathered around her. They did their best to cheer her up.

'Don't worry, Snow White,' they said. 'We'll take care of you.' Snow White was delighted to find that she had so many friends.

'The first thing to do,' said a squirrel, 'is to find you a nice place where you can live.'

At that, all the animals cried out: 'Let's take her to
the dwarfs' house!'
'What is the dwarfs' house?' asked Snow White.
But the animals, all chirping and chattering
together, only laughed. They wanted it to be a
surprise.
Led by a little bird flying from tree branch to tree
branch, they set off through the forest. Presently,
they came to a clearing. Pointing, the animals
shouted:
'Princess, here is your new palace!'

19

Snow White opened the door of the little cottage and gasped.
'It's very, very dirty for a palace!' she said.
'That's true!' chorused the animals. 'The dwarfs aren't very tidy, you know. And they are out at work all day long.'
'But what will they think if they find me here when they come back?'
'They'll think you are the most beautiful Princess in the world!'
Snow White blushed. 'I don't know about that,' she said. 'But I think I'd better tidy things up. Now, where is the broom. . . .'

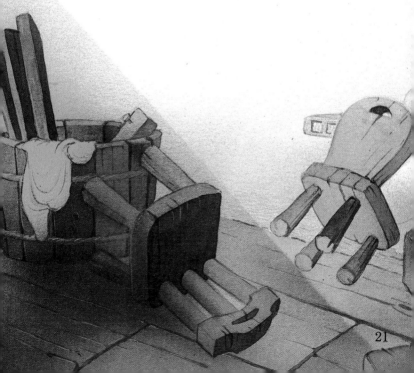

With some help from the
forest animals, Snow White
soon had the cottage looking
bright and shiny.
Upstairs she found a
bedroom and in it were seven
little beds in a line. Each one
had a name over it: Dopey,
Grumpy, Sneezy, Doc,
Sleepy, Bashful and Happy.
What strange names, she
said to herself.
Then suddenly she felt very
tired. She stretched out
across the seven beds, pulled
the blankets over her, and
immediately fell fast asleep.

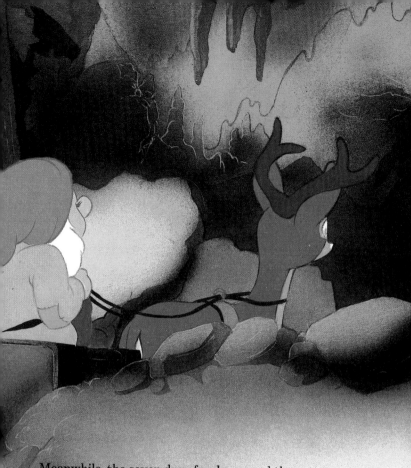

Meanwhile, the seven dwarfs who owned the cottage were just finishing their work in the mine where they searched for diamonds.

'That's enough for me today,' said Grumpy, throwing down his pick-axe.

Sleepy said with a big yawn: 'Yes. It's time I was in bed.'

Bashful said: 'I'm not really sure, but I suppose you're right.'

'A tisshoo!' went Sneezy.

Doc counted up the number of diamonds they had found that day.

And Happy and Dopey began to sing.

As they set off home, the dwarfs sang in time to Happy's conducting.

'*Heigh-ho, heigh-ho,*
It's home from work we go!'

Suddenly they all stopped and the words of the song died on their lips.

For there in the clearing before them was their little cottage. And the windows were all lit up.

'Advance slowly!' whispered Doc. 'A robber must have broken into our home!'

The dwarfs crept on tip-toe towards the cottage, opened the door, and jumped back in amazement.

Instead of all the dust and disorder they had left behind them, everything was bright and shiny!

Doc frowned. 'Let's look upstairs,' he whispered.

A big lump lay under the blankets across their seven beds. 'Someone is hiding under those blankets!' cried Doc. He raised his pick-axe. 'Come out, whoever you are!'

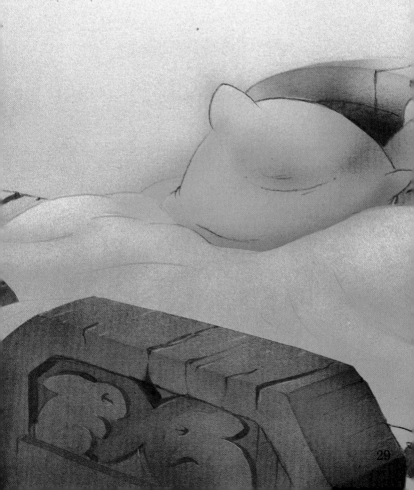

Snow White, wakened by all the noise, sat up.

'Well, that's a rather pretty robber!' laughed Happy.

'I'm not a robber,' explained the Princess. 'My name is Snow White.'

Doc said: 'I think you'd better explain, miss. First, what are you doing in our cottage asleep in our beds?'

So Snow White told her story.

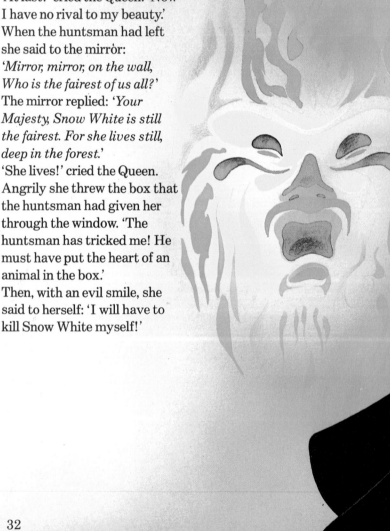

Back at the royal palace the huntsman fell
on his knees before the Queen.
'Your Majesty, I have killed Snow White!'
he said. 'And just as you ordered, I have
put her heart in this box.'
'At last!' cried the Queen. 'Now
I have no rival to my beauty.'
When the huntsman had left
she said to the mirror:
'*Mirror, mirror, on the wall,*
Who is the fairest of us all?'
The mirror replied: '*Your*
Majesty, Snow White is still
the fairest. For she lives still,
deep in the forest.'
'She lives!' cried the Queen.
Angrily she threw the box that
the huntsman had given her
through the window. 'The
huntsman has tricked me! He
must have put the heart of an
animal in the box.'
Then, with an evil smile, she
said to herself: 'I will have to
kill Snow White myself!'

33

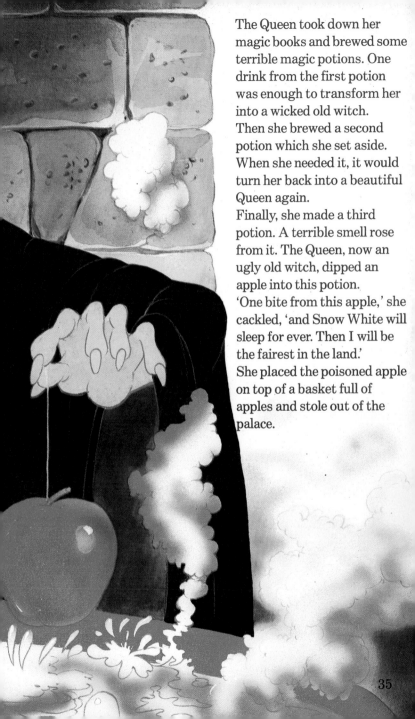

The Queen took down her
magic books and brewed some
terrible magic potions. One
drink from the first potion
was enough to transform her
into a wicked old witch.
Then she brewed a second
potion which she set aside.
When she needed it, it would
turn her back into a beautiful
Queen again.
Finally, she made a third
potion. A terrible smell rose
from it. The Queen, now an
ugly old witch, dipped an
apple into this potion.
'One bite from this apple,' she
cackled, 'and Snow White will
sleep for ever. Then I will be
the fairest in the land.'
She placed the poisoned apple
on top of a basket full of
apples and stole out of the
palace.

When Snow White finished telling the seven dwarfs how she had been turned into a servant, and how her step-mother the Queen had ordered the huntsman to kill her, they all had tears in their eyes – except, of course, Happy.

'Now that Snow White is safe with us, she can be our big sister!' he cried.

'Just a moment,' said Doc. 'Princess, do you want seven poor dwarfs for your brothers?'

'Of course!' said Snow White. 'But on one condition. You all need a good wash. You must start by washing your hands.'

The dwarfs stretched out their hands for Snow White to inspect.

'Come on!' she cried. 'Everyone to the fountain!'

That evening seven smart,
clean and well-washed
dwarfs played music while
Snow White danced merrily.

Meanwhile, the Witch-Queen took a rowing boat moored alongside the palace and rowed along the river that flowed through the forest. In the boat she had her basket of apples, with the poisoned apple on top of the pile.

At dawn the next day the dwarfs prepared to go to work in their mine.

They lined up in front of Snow White so that she could give each one a kiss. Bashful looked very bashful when Snow White kissed him, and Grumpy looked grumpier than ever. But Happy and Dopey just laughed!

While the dwarfs were at work Snow White got on with the housework. After tidying up she decided to bake a big pie for supper. The birds and animals came into the kitchen from the forest and talked to her while she worked.

Outside the door an old lady came hobbling through the forest. Her back was bent with age and she seemed hardly able to walk. Snow White felt very sorry for her.

'Good morning, madam,' she said. 'Can I help you in any way?'

'I need nothing,' croaked the old woman. 'But you look like a nice young girl, so here's a present for you, dearie.'

So saying, she took a bright red juicy apple from the basket of apples that she was carrying and offered it to Snow White.

The birds of the forest, who saw what was happening, flew through the trees crying at the tops of their voices.

'Come quickly! *Quickly!*'

The fawns, the squirrels, the rabbits and even the tortoise hurried towards the cottage in the clearing.

But when they arrived it was too late.

Snow White had already started to eat the poisoned apple!

What a commotion there was then among the animals! They scampered through the trees to the mine where the dwarfs worked and, breathlessly, tried to show them that they must hurry back at once to their cottage.

'What's all this about?' asked Doc, who understood some of the animals' language. 'Snow White . . . a witch . . . a poisoned apple . . .?

The seven dwarfs threw down their pick-axes and ran back to their cottage as fast as they could.

The dwarfs arrived just in time to see the Witch-Queen
sneaking out of their front door.
Poor Snow White lay on the floor, the poisoned apple still
in her hand.
Riding on the backs of the fawns, the dwarfs raced after
the Witch-Queen.
They drove her this way and that, deeper and deeper into
the forest.

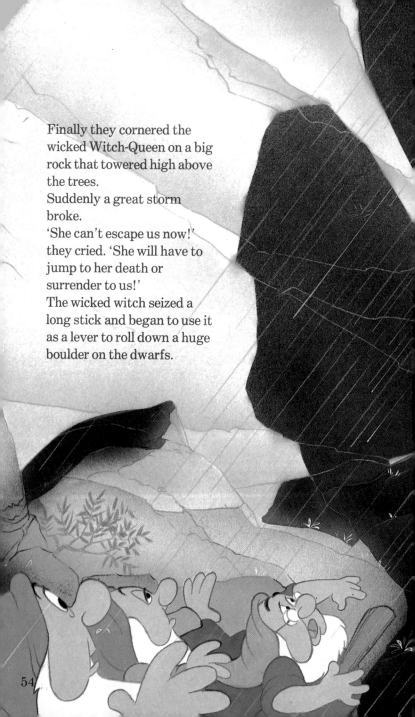

Finally they cornered the
wicked Witch-Queen on a big
rock that towered high above
the trees.
Suddenly a great storm
broke.
'She can't escape us now!'
they cried. 'She will have to
jump to her death or
surrender to us!'
The wicked witch seized a
long stick and began to use it
as a lever to roll down a huge
boulder on the dwarfs.

The rain came pouring down and suddenly a vivid flash of
lightning struck the rock where the Witch-Queen was
standing. She screamed, and as the thunder rolled across the
sky, she fell to her doom below.
'She will never poison anyone again!'
cried the dwarfs.

But it seemed that the poor dwarfs were too late to help Snow White. They lifted her lifeless body from the floor of their cottage. She was so beautiful, however, that they could not bear to part with her.

So they built her a coffin of glass and gold and heaped fresh flowers all around it. Then day and night they knelt before the coffin and kept watch over their beloved Princess.

They gave her so much love that the strength of it was felt all through the forest. So it was that Prince Charming, riding through the forest one day, was drawn to the dwarfs' cottage and saw, in the clearing, the glass and gold coffin of Snow White.

He dismounted from his horse and walked towards the Princess.

'How beautiful she is!' he breathed.

The Prince leaned over the Princess and fell more deeply in love with her than ever. Kneeling beside the coffin, he could not resist kissing her.

Snow White sat up, blinked her eyes, and smiled. She wasn't dead after all. The Prince's kiss had broken the Queen's evil spell!

As the dwarfs danced with joy, the Prince carried Snow White off to his castle, where they lived happily ever after.